Cupcake Surprise!

by LYNN MASLEN KERTELL
illustrated by SUE HENDRA

SCHOLASTIC INC.

ISBN 978-1-338-80509-3

10 9 8 7 6 5 4 3 2 1   22 23 24 25 26

Printed in the U.S.A.   40
This edition first printing 2022

It is Dad's birthday.

What will Jack and Anna give to Dad?

Will they make a card?
Will they jot a note?
Will they sing a song?

Jack and Anna will
make cupcakes for Dad.

Cupcakes will be a big surprise.

Anna has the cookbook.

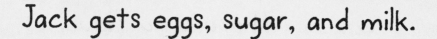

Jack gets eggs, sugar, and milk.

Oh, no. There is no flour.

That is not a good surprise.

Jack and Anna go to the store.

At the store they get flour.
They get cookies, too.

Jack puts in flour and sugar.
Anna puts in milk, butter, and eggs.

Stir it up, Jack!

Uh-oh! The cookies fall in.
That is a surprise.

They mix in the cookies.

Oh, no! Chips fall in.
That is a surprise.

They mix in the chips.

Stir it all up, Jack.

Buddy wants to help, too.

Mom puts the cupcakes in to bake.

Jack and Anna watch the cupcakes.
Buddy watches, too.

Yum!

24

The cupcakes look good.

Happy birthday, Dad!

Here are your birthday cupcakes.

Surprise!
These cupcakes taste great!

Cupcake Surprise!

With a grown-up helping, you can make a Cupcake Surprise! Here is the recipe.

Ingredients:

Cookies to make 1 1/2 cups cookie pieces
    (about 15 cookies)

1 box white cake mix, plus additional ingredients
    listed on box

3/4 cup chocolate chips

Frosting to top cupcakes

Directions:

1. Ask a grown-up to preheat the oven to the temperature listed on your cake mix box.

2. Line 24 muffin cups with cupcake liners.

Directions continued on next page.

3. Break up the cookies: Smash the cookies with a potato masher, or put the cookies in a zip-top bag and gently crush them with a rolling pin. If you have a food processor, ask a grown-up to help process the cookies.

4. Make the cake batter, following the directions on the box.

5. Stir in the chocolate chips and 1 cup of the cookie pieces. Divide the batter among the muffin cups.

6. Ask a grown-up to help you put the cupcakes in the oven. Bake according to the directions on the cake mix box.

7. Ask a grown-up to help you take the cupcakes out of the oven. When they are cool, frost them and top with the remaining cookie pieces.

BOB BOOKS®

The Complete Bob Books® Series

READING READINESS

MY FIRST BOB BOOKS® PRE-READING SKILLS

MY FIRST BOB BOOKS® ALPHABET

STAGE 1: STARTING TO READ

SET 1 BEGINNING READERS

MORE BEGINNING READERS

FIRST STORIES

RHYMING WORDS

STAGE 2: EMERGING READER

ADVANCING BEGINNERS

SIGHT WORDS KINDERGARTEN

ANIMAL STORIES

SIGHT WORDS FIRST GRADE

STAGE 3: DEVELOPING READER

WORD FAMILIES

COMPLEX WORDS

LONG VOWELS

SCHOLASTIC